Fashion Fairy Princess

Matt Bleach

Thanks fairy much Catherine Coe!

First published in the UK in 2014 by Scholastic Children's Books
An imprint of Scholastic Ltd
Euston House, 24 Eversholt Street
London, NW1 1DB, UK
Registered office: Westfield Road, Southam, Warwickshire, CV47 0RA
SCHOLASTIC and associated logos are trademarks and/or registered
trademarks of Scholastic Inc.

Text copyright © Scholastic Ltd, 2014
Cover copyright © Pixie Potts, Beehive Illustration Agency, 2014
Inside illustration copyright © David Shephard, The Bright Agency, 2014

The right of Poppy Collins to be identified as the author
of this work has been asserted by her.

ISBN 978 1407 14523 5

Printed and bound by CPI Group (UK) Ltd, Croydon, CR0 4YY
Papers used by Scholastic Children's Books are made
from wood grown in sustainable forests.

1 3 5 7 9 10 8 6 4 2

This is a work of fiction. Names, characters, places,
incidents and dialogues are products of the author's imagination
or are used fictitiously. Any resemblance to actual people, living
or dead, events or locales is entirely coincidental.

www.scholastic.co.uk
www.fashionfairyprincess.com

Fashion Fairy Princess

Willa
in Jewel Forest

POPPY COLLINS

■SCHOLASTIC

Dream
Mountain

Jewel Forest

Sparkle
City

Star
Valley

River
Sapphire

Shimmer Island

Glitter Ocean

Welcome to the world of the fashion fairy princesses! Join Willa and friends on their magical adventures in fairyland.

They can't wait to explore

Jewel Forest!

Can you?

Chapter 1

Willa fluttered down to her tree house in the opal-oak tree. She'd been out collecting sapphire berries all morning. They'd just come into season so she was planning on making some jam. She heaved the sack off her shoulder and was about to push open her door when she saw something poking out of her walnut-shell letter box.

"Ooh, I wasn't expecting any post," she

said to herself. "I wonder what it is!"

As Willa pulled out the light blue envelope, she heard someone behind her.

"Hi, Willa!" called Pip in her tiny lilting voice. She stood waving in the arched door of her tree house. Pip lived in the neighbouring opal-oak tree to Willa. "Do you fancy a cup of beechnut tea? I've just made a pot."

"That would be lovely – thank you, Pip. All that flying about in the forest has made me thirsty!" Willa grinned at her friend and fluttered on to the silvery branch that led to Pip's doorway. She could open the letter while she drank her tea. Willa ducked down to get through Pip's archway. Pip was the smallest forest fairy, and she had a tiny home to match! It was very pretty inside, with knotted beams studded with rubies, and a diamond-daisy rug on the floor.

Inside, Pip poured the sparkling beechnut tea into sugar-cane cups while

Willa read the elegant gold handwriting on the envelope:

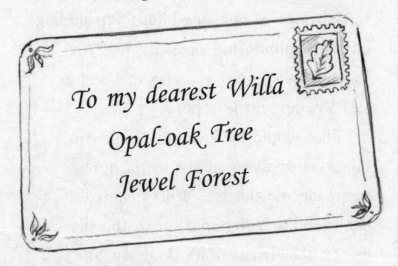

To my dearest Willa
Opal-oak Tree
Jewel Forest

She tucked her long dark hair behind her pointy ears before sliding a finger under the envelope's flap.

"You've got a letter?" Pip asked as Willa began to read. "It looks important!"

Willa looked up, her big brown eyes shining below her fringe. "It is!" she cried. "It's from my friend Topaz, who lives in Sparkle City. She's getting married – and she's coming back to Jewel Forest for the wedding!"

"Oh, wow," murmured Pip. "A wedding. In Jewel Forest!"

"That's not all," Willa continued. "She's asked me to be her flower girl!"

Pip fluttered towards Willa and squeezed her in a hug. "Congratulations!"

Willa frowned. "But I've never been a flower girl before — what do I have to do?"

"Well, it means that you're a special part of the wedding — you'll walk behind Topaz down the aisle and wear a beautiful dress. Sometimes flower girls help with the preparations, too. Does Topaz say anything about that?"

Willa's hands shook with excitement as she read the letter over again. "Yes, here — look."

As you're already in Jewel Forest, would you mind helping with the preparations, dear Willa? I'll need a cake and decorations, but you don't need to worry about my dress. I've had it specially made in Sparkle City and it's being delivered to your house by magic-express fairy mail. Thank you so fairy

much, Willa. I can't wait to have you as
my flower girl!
    With lots of love,
    Topaz xxx

Willa blew out a sigh of relief. "Thank goodness she hasn't asked me to organize her dress — it's the most important part of a wedding! I'd be too worried I'd mess it up!"

"Arranging the decorations and the cake sounds like fun, though," said Pip. "What will you start with?"

Willa took a sip of the sweet, nutty tea and looked back down at the letter. "Well, the wedding's only two days away — so I think I'd better begin with the cake!" Their friend Blossom owned the bakery in Jewel Forest, and she was always busy making delicious treats for the forest fairies. "I hope Blossom will have time to do it!"

"Do you want me to help you write a list of things to do?" Pip offered.

Willa shook her head, picked up her tea and drank it in one long gulp. "Thanks, but I'd better get going. There's so much to sort out!"

"If you're sure," said Pip. "I wish I could come and help, but I've got to wait for my honey-blossom bread that's baking in the oven."

"I thought I could smell something delicious." Willa winked. "Save me a slice for later!" She jumped up and, with a swish of her polka-dot dress, flew through the door.

Pip waved goodbye, grinning at her impulsive friend. Willa could never sit around for very long. "Good luck, Willa!"

she cried, as Willa's pink-tinged wings
disappeared from sight.

Chapter 2

Willa zoomed along the forest fairy skyway. The skyway was a network of leaf bridges that were rebuilt every spring. The bridges weaved high up above the forest ground, connecting all the houses and shops – as well as the beautiful Tree Palace, where the Jewel Forest royalty lived. Willa never got tired of flying through the forest, seeing the gleaming trees sparkling in the sunshine.

But today she didn't have time to admire the prettiness of her home. She had work to do! She squeezed past a group of candy-tufted tree squirrels carrying bags of nuts on the tips of their pink fluffy tails, then zipped in front of a blue-winged fairy pushing a barrow of poppy pearls. At the Tree Palace crossroads she took the bridge to her right, but she was so focused on getting to the bakery that she wasn't paying enough attention. She flew into a fairy coming the other way, knocking her off balance.

"I'm sorry!" Willa called over her shoulder. "It's just that I'm in a hurry!" She widened her eyes at the fairy she'd bumped into, who was adjusting the tiara in her nut-brown hair. It was her friend Princess Primrose! Willa zoomed back. "Oh, Primrose, are you OK?"

"Where are you going in such a rush?" Primrose asked, her hazel eyes wide.

Willa was relieved to see she had a smile on her face. "I'm *so* sorry, Primrose!" she cried. "It's just that I've got lots to do — you see, Topaz is getting married and she asked me to be her flower girl, and the wedding's in two days, here in Jewel Forest, and I've got to sort out the cake and the decorations and—"

Primrose put a hand on Willa's arm. "Whoa, calm down, Willa — you'll run out of fairy breath if you talk much faster!" she said in her calm, delicate voice. "Maybe I can help you? I was heading back to the Tree Palace to work on my spider-silk embroidery – but I can do that another day."

Primrose's offer suddenly made Willa feel much better. "Are you sure? It would be great to have some help choosing the cake. I have no idea about it – I've never been to a wedding!"

"Well, then, I insist!" said Primrose. "And anyway, I'd never turn down a chance to visit Blossom and taste her amazing cakes!" She gave Willa a wink. "Come on, I know a shortcut through the silver-willow tree!" She pointed to a tree a little way ahead, and the two fairies zoomed up towards it.

Willa stared at the tree, wondering how they would ever get through it. Its long silvery leaves trailed down like a shimmery curtain. But once she'd parted back the branches, she wasn't sure she wanted to leave. It was magical, with rays of sunshine bouncing off the thin leaves, casting silver light everywhere. Primrose weaved in and out through the branches, pulling Willa along by her hand. In no time, they'd reached the other side.

"Here we are!" Primrose grinned at Willa. They had emerged back on to the

skyway and were now standing in front
of Blossom's Bakery. In less than three
flutters of their wings, they were inside
the bakery, sniffing in delight at the sweet
smells in the air.

Cake stands filled the window, and the
counter and shelves were all loaded with
gorgeous cakes and sweet treats. There
were orange-opal cakes and star-cream
buns, and sparkle muffins with rainbow
icing. On the counter stood a row of
jars filled with giant cookies, chocolate-
almond shimmers, and macaroons in every
colour you could imagine. *Wow*, Willa
thought, *Blossom is so talented!*

But where *was* Blossom? Willa tiptoed
to look over the counter, and found
Blossom kneeling down and staring
through the window of her large oven.

"Hi, Blossom, are you OK?" Willa asked.

The blonde fairy jumped up, her
green eyes wide in surprise. "Oh, I'm
sorry Willa, – I didn't hear you come
in! I was watching the cinnamon-curly-
cream buns. They're very difficult to get
right – one second too long and they
fall as flat as pancakes. And I'm terrible at
remembering to check them!"

"I bet they're worth the trouble,
though," said Primrose.

Blossom nodded. "They're one of my bestsellers – in fact, I'd just run out of them. I hope you didn't want any? This batch will take a while to cool." She bent down and pulled the baking tray out of the oven with rose-petal oven gloves. A delicious smell of cinnamon filled the air.

Willa shook her head. "No, not today, thanks. But I have come to ask you a huge favour, Blossom. You see, my fairy friend Topaz is getting married in Jewel Forest in two days' time, and I need to organize a cake for her wedding. I know it's short notice but—"

"Of course I'll do it!" Blossom spun on the spot, her wavy blonde hair billowing around her and her pale green wings quivering in excitement. "I love making wedding cakes most of all!"

"Really?" Willa asked. "Oh, Blossom, that would be wonderful. How can I ever thank you?"

Blossom winked. "As long as I can come to the wedding, I'll be happy."

"Of course! The whole forest is invited!" Willa told her.

"Wow – then we'd better start making plans for a gigantic cake!" Primrose added.

Blossom took a gold-leaf notepad from the polished walnut counter. "Primrose, you're right – there's no time to waste." Blossom began sketching out cake designs. She gave Willa and Primrose violet-fizz macaroons to eat as they watched. The little purple biscuits were melt-in-your-mouth delicious.

Soon, Blossom had designed a multi-layered wedding cake. It was in the shape

of a tree, with a chocolate-cake trunk,
peppermint-cream leaves and sparkly
edible flowers from the Twinkle Tree in
Star Valley.

"What do you think, Primrose – is it
right for a forest fairy wedding?" asked
Willa. It looked wonderful to her, and she
knew it would taste amazing too.

"It's perfect." Primrose nodded. "I'm
sure Topaz will love it!"

Chapter 3

"So, what's next?" asked Primrose as they waved goodbye to Blossom and fluttered back to the sparkling skyway. Fairies and forest animals skipped by in front of them. "Oh look, there's Catkin!"

Willa turned her head and saw Catkin's curly red hair bouncing along the opposite bridge. She grinned as she saw Primrose and Willa waving, and flew over.

"Hi, Willa. Hi, Primrose! Have you just been to the bakery?"

"Yes, to order a wedding cake!" Willa said. She told Catkin about Topaz's wedding in Jewel Forest.

"Oh, that sounds wonderful," said Catkin. "Weddings are always so much fun. But of course there's a lot to organize, too! Can I help you with anything?"

"Well, we're just about to fly

down to the forest floor to ask the animals if they'll give me a hand with decorations." Willa hoped her animal friends would help make the wedding beautiful, with bunting and lanterns and petal confetti.

"Good idea! And you've got the cake sorted. What about the music? Is there going to be a band?" Catkin asked.

Willa put a hand to her forehead. "Music! I hadn't even thought about that!" Maybe she *should* have written a list, like Pip had suggested.

"Oh yes — it wouldn't

be a proper wedding without dancing," Primrose agreed.

Willa flapped her wings in panic. "But where will I get a band from? I can't sing – or play an instrument." She looked at Catkin and Primrose hopefully. "Can you?"

Her two friends shook their heads. "My singing's worse than a tree squirrel's!" said Primrose. "And I never learnt to play anything at school – not even the bamboo flute. When I tried, my fingers got all muddled up!"

Catkin put an arm around Willa. "I'm sorry, but I'd be no good either. I love to dance, but the only place I sing is in my sunbeam shower!"

What am I going to do? Willa thought. *I can't let Topaz down!*

Deep in thought, the three fairies

fluttered along the delicate leafy skyway, which twinkled with light green crystals.

"So the wedding is the day after tomorrow?" Catkin asked.

"Yes, and the—"

Bee-coo-be-be-cookoo! Coo be-be-bebe!

Willa's reply was drowned out by a nest of purple sparrows. The pretty birds sang over each other, louder and louder, as if they were having a competition.

Willa spun round and stared at the sparrows.

"That's it – we'll have a competition!"

"What do you mean?"

asked Primrose, looking from Willa to the birds and back to Willa again.

"We'll hold auditions for a fairy band! There must be plenty of fairies and creatures in the forest who *can* sing and play an instrument. . ."

Primrose clapped her hands together. "Oh, that's *such* a good idea!"

Suddenly Willa's smile turned into a deep frown. "But I need to go and tell everyone about it — and I can't do that *and* arrange the wedding decorations. We'll have to have the auditions tomorrow to be ready in time! Oh, there's *so* much to do!"

"But we can help you!" said Catkin. "There's no need to do everything on your own. Why don't I go and spread the word about the fairy band auditions while you and Primrose speak to the tree squirrels about the decorations."

"Really?" asked Willa. "Are you sure?"

"Of course! And if I ask everyone I meet to pass the message on, the whole forest will know about the auditions in no time!"

"That's a great plan," said Primrose. "We can tell everyone we meet, too!"

Willa felt a lot more cheerful. Thank fairyness for her friends!

Catkin grinned and began zooming back along the sparkling skyway. Willa saw her stop to talk to a group of fairies from the cherry-jewel tree, who all nodded and smiled. Catkin was doing a great job already!

There really is an AWFUL lot to organize for a wedding, thought Willa as she and Primrose flew along the gleaming green bridge. *Cake, decorations, music. . . But at least I don't have to worry about the dress!*

Chapter 4

Willa woke with a start. She sat up in her palm-leaf hammock, hoping she hadn't overslept. But it was OK – the sun was only just rising over the horizon, casting a gorgeous pinky glow over the whole forest.

She yawned, stretched out her pink wings, and fluttered over to the window to admire the magical sunrise. As she looked outside, she spotted a note pinned

to a branch nearby. Willa quickly fluttered
out of the doorway and plucked it off.

Good morning, Willa!
    Everything's set for the band
auditions. Meet me in the Great Wood
Hall!
    Catkin x

Before long, Willa was standing in the

huge carved room of Great Wood Hall. It was beautiful. Sunlight streamed in through the jewel-glass windows, shining multicoloured rays on to the wooden floor. At the door stood a queue of forest fairies and animals chattering nervously, all waiting to audition.

Catkin was already sitting down on a golden toadstool seat in front of the stage.

Willa flew over to join her. "Hi, Catkin. Thank you so much for arranging the auditions! Please will you help me judge them?"

Catkin looked up, her blue eyes sparkling. "I was hoping you'd ask! I prepared audition sheets for us."

She passed a piece of reed-paper to Willa, and Willa grinned at her super-organized friend. The sheet had one column for names and one for comments. "Ready?" Willa asked Catkin, who nodded. "Please could the first contestant enter?" Willa called across the room.

The fairies did a double take. Pip was climbing up the stairs to the stage!

"Hello, Pip – I didn't know you could

strument!" said Catkin.

looked back at them shyly, pushing
cute bobbed hair behind her pointy
ears. "Um . . . well . . . I can't," she said
in a tiny voice barely audible in the great
hall. "But I like to sing."

Willa was surprised – she had never
heard Pip sing before. The tiny fairy had
such a quiet voice that Willa couldn't

imagine it! Pip shuffled up to the yellow bellflower microphone and took a deep breath.

What came out was a magical, wonderful sound. Pip's voice was soft but vibrant, beautifully in tune, and it reached every single high note. Through the bellflower microphone, her voice rang clearly around the high-ceilinged hall. When Pip reached the last line, a tingle shot up Willa's spine. Her friend's voice was incredible. She *had* to be in the fairy band!

Willa picked up her beeswax pen and wrote a big "YES" in the comments box. She glanced over at Primrose's sheet – she'd jotted exactly the same!

"Thank you, Pip," said Catkin.

"Can you wait outside the hall?" asked Willa. "We'll call you back when we announce the chosen band members."

Pip nodded and jumped down from the stage. "Yes," she said, her voice tiny again without the microphone.

Next to audition was a tree squirrel who played an acorn guitar, followed by a flute-playing fairy. A cricket played a web-string harp, a trio of hummingbirds hummed, and two fairy twins played trumpet flowers. The queue went on and on. It felt like most of the forest

had come to audition – even the
sparrows who'd given Willa the idea.

It was almost midday when the last fairy
walked on stage. She carried an entire
acorn-nut drum set with her and began
setting it out. When she turned round,
Willa saw it was Nutmeg, Primrose's sister!

"I didn't know she played the drums,"
said Catkin.

"Nor did I," Willa replied. "But I bet
Primrose does – it must be noisy for her,
as her bedroom's right next door!"

Catkin pulled a face. "Poor Primrose!"

But when Nutmeg started playing, they
both sat up straight and listened properly.
Nutmeg's drumming was lyrical and
gentle, and she tapped a catchy rhythm
with her maple-twig drumsticks as if she'd
been playing for many years.

"I take it back," Catkin whispered to

Willa. "She's fantastic!"

Nutmeg finished playing and rushed over to Willa and Catkin, her freckled cheeks flushed pink. "Was I OK? I really want to be in the fairy band at the wedding!"

Catkin smiled. "We're about to announce who will play in the band – so you'll soon find out! Could you ask everyone else to come back in, please?"

The enthusiastic little fairy ran out of the doorway, returning moments later with the rest of the forest fairies and animals in tow. They gathered on the stage in the Great Wood Hall, all nervously jumping about from foot to foot.

"Thank you, everyone, for auditioning," Willa began. "You were amazing."

"We're just sorry we can't put you all in the band," added Catkin. "Willa will now read out the names of the band members."

Willa cleared her throat, looked down at their notes, and began.

"The singer will be Pip."

The little fairy squealed with delight, and a few of the other fairies hugged her.

"George the cricket will be on the harp, and the twins Juniper and Jasmine on trumpets. Backing vocals will be the sparrow sisters, and finally, on the drums . . . Nutmeg!"

Nutmeg burst to the front of the stage, bouncing up and

down. "Really – you've chosen me? Oh, thank you!" She leapt from the platform, fluttered over to Willa and Catkin and threw her arms around them.

"We thought you played the drums beautifully," said Catkin. "I can't believe we haven't heard you before."

Just then the hall door creaked open. "I'm sorry, but the auditions are over," Willa called out.

"I'm not here for the auditions," said a giggling voice. "I'm here for my wedding!"

Chapter 5

Willa gasped. Topaz! She jumped up
and zoomed over to her friend as the
strawberry-blonde fairy flew through
the doorway, her blue wings fluttering
crazily.

"Oh, I'm so excited!" she cried as she
hugged Willa. "It looks like you've been
very busy!" Topaz spun round, her face
alight. As she moved, her pink heart-
print silk dress floated about and her

cute red peep-toe
heels tapped
on the floor.
Topaz owned
a clothes
shop, Sparkle
Sensations, in
Sparkle City,
so she always
wore gorgeous
outfits.

"We have!" replied Willa, a beam
stretching across her face. "But I couldn't
have done it without my friends." She
guided Topaz over to Catkin.

"This is Catkin," she said, introducing
her friends. "We've just chosen the
wedding band together!"

"Oh wow – a band, how fabulous!"
Topaz waved at the band members

standing on the stage. "I can't wait to hear them."

The band looked nervous at this — they hadn't practised together at all yet! Catkin stepped forward. "We'll save that as a surprise for tomorrow, if that's OK, Topaz?"

"Of course! I'm sure you'll be wonderful!" she said to the band. Then she turned to Willa. "So where do you think we should have the wedding ceremony? Right here in the Great Wood Hall?"

"Actually, I have another idea," Willa said with a wink. "Let me show you. . ."

Willa took Topaz's hand and they flew out of the hall, while Catkin stayed behind to help the band practise for the following day.

Moments later, Willa and Topaz were

on the skyway, just above the forest floor. Willa told Topaz to close her eyes as they got closer. "OK, just a little further," said Willa, guiding her friend. "Now open!"

Willa held her breath nervously. She so hoped Topaz would like it! Topaz blinked her eyes open. They were above a clearing on the forest floor that had been carpeted in thousands of pale pink rose petals. The clearing was edged with sparkling willow trees, their silvery drooping leaves shimmering like a giant curtain, lighting up the whole clearing. Topaz looked down and gasped – flower-shaped lanterns hung from golden spiders' webs.

"When the ceremony ends and the sun goes down, the lanterns will light up in all the colours of the rainbow!" Willa explained. "Oh look, there's Conker. Let me introduce you to him."

The fairies zipped over to Conker, a pink tree squirrel who was hanging up wild-flower bunting at the other side of the clearing, his back to them. He finished hooking a stem of lavender over a willow branch and turned round. "Oh, hello, Willa."

"Hi, Conker – the clearing looks beautiful! A real wedding wonderland. I'd like to introduce you to Topaz, the fairy bride!"

Topaz held out her hand, which was covered in gemstone rings. "Conker, it's lovely to meet you. Thank you for all you've done – I couldn't have dreamt of anything better."

Conker shook Topaz's hand with a fluffy pink paw. "It's a pleasure – a wedding in Jewel Forest is a very special event!

We squirrels can't wait for tomorrow."

"Well, thank you again, Conker – and I'm looking forward to saying thank you to everyone when I see them tomorrow." Topaz turned to Willa. "You've done an amazing job of the preparations, Willa. I am *so* grateful! Now I can't wait any longer to see my dress! Isn't it beautiful? I had it made specially, using fabric woven with fairy dust!"

Willa's heart plummeted to her fairy feet. The wedding dress – it hadn't arrived yet! She stood in front of Topaz, speechless.

"What's the matter, Willa? It is OK, isn't it? Or do you hate it? I knew I shouldn't have asked for so many jewels on it. . ."

"It's not that," Willa began. "It's just that . . . well . . . I haven't seen it. Um, I mean, it hasn't actually arrived. . ."

"But it was meant to get here yesterday. I sent it by magic-express fairy mail! Are you sure? You wouldn't miss it – it's in a huge silver box with a pale pink bow. . ."

Willa shook her head sadly. "I'm so sorry, Topaz. It must have got lost in the fairy mail."

Topaz slumped down on the petal carpet, pretty petals bouncing up around her. "Well, that's it, then," she sobbed, taking a lace-edged handkerchief from her pocket and dabbing at the fat drops of tears that rushed down her cheeks. "I can't get married without a dress. We'll have to –" She blew her nose loudly and let out another big sob – "cancel the wedding. . ."

"What?! No, we can't do that!" Willa said, shocked. She sat down cross-legged

opposite Topaz and
put her hands on her
shoulders. "There's
got to be something
we can do – and
as your flower
girl, I just
won't let the
wedding be
ruined
that
easily."

Topaz looked up
at Willa and wiped away more tears.
"Really?" she said, her blue eyes wide.

"Yes, *really*," Willa replied. "Just leave it
with me!"

Chapter 6

All the way back to the Great Wood Hall, Willa's head was buzzing like a beehive. She'd left Topaz with Conker and the other squirrels – she hoped they'd cheer her up while Willa worked out what to do about the dress. By the time she'd arrived at the hall, she'd thought of a plan – but she had no idea whether it would work in time!

"Catkin!" she called as she burst

through the doorway. "I need your help!"

The band screeched to a halt mid-song, and Catkin spun round with a frown. "Willa, that was the best run-through yet! Whatever's the matter?"

"It's Topaz's dress – it hasn't arrived, and she's saying that she'll have to cancel the wedding!"

Catkin's mouth fell open. "What? That's terrible."

"But I have an idea. I just need your

help. Meet me in the entrance hall of the palace? I need to go and tell the others."

Before Catkin could ask what Willa was planning, the determined fairy had already left the hall. "You'll have to finish practising on your own," Catkin told the band. "But don't worry, you're doing brilliantly!"

Catkin fluttered out of the Great Wood Hall and into the hollow trunk of the Tree Palace. The sun shone down right from the very top of the tree, lighting up the inside. She wound her way down the staircase carved into the trunk, passing beautiful engravings of forest fairy scenes on the walls. When she arrived at the grand entrance hall, Willa was already there, talking to Primrose.

"Of course you can use my room," said Primrose, "but can I help, too?"

"Absolutely – I'm going to need all the help I can get!" Willa turned to Catkin. "Oh, Catkin, thank you for coming so quickly! I have a plan, but we need to get started right away. Let's go to Primrose's bedroom – everyone can meet us there."

Primrose fluttered over to the smooth wall of the tree trunk, running her hands over the wood. She found the pointy, forest-fairy-ear-shaped knot she was looking for, put her mouth close and whispered something. A wooden panel in the wall suddenly slid back and revealed a secret staircase inside. "This will take us straight to my room!"

Willa grinned – she loved the magic of the Tree Palace. The three fairies stepped inside the secret passageway. The stairs were lit with gleaming pink diamond nuts, so it was easy to find their way. Soon they

stepped out into Primrose's bedroom.

If you could call it a bedroom! The circular room was almost as big as the Great Wood Hall – which was why Willa had asked if they could use it. Primrose's large oak desk next to the leaf-shaped windows would be perfect.

Willa explained her plan. "I've asked some magpies and hummingbirds to collect the nicest leaves from the forest, and the moth family to bring some jewel-moth silk. I also asked Poppy and

Orla and Daisy to pick some jewels from the trees, and when Blossom's finished icing the last layer of the wedding cake, she's going to help us decorate."

"Decorate what?" asked Catkin, looking confused.

"Topaz's new wedding dress!" Willa grabbed a cherry-blossom notepad from Primrose's desk. "That's what all those things are for."

"Oh, Willa, you are clever," said Primrose. "But do you think we'll get it made it time?"

At that moment, Blossom appeared through the doorway. "When Willa's this determined," she said, "she can get *anything* done!"

But Primrose is right to be worried, Willa thought, looking at Primrose's pink cuckoo clock on the wall. They only had the afternoon – not long at all!

Soon, Primrose's huge room was full
of fairies and creatures bringing materials
for the new dress. Everyone rushed
about, and Catkin thought it was rather
chaotic – but, Willa seemed to know
what she was doing!

Willa stood at Primrose's desk,
directing the mice to weave together
the beautiful mulberry and laurel leaves.
The hummingbirds held the leaves in

place with their beaks as the mice did the sewing. Then Poppy, Orla and Daisy arrived with bamboo baskets full of glistening gems.

"Perfect!" Willa cried. She began sorting through the gems and arranging them into piles. "These are for the train of the dress," she explained to Primrose, "and these are for the neckline and sleeves. Oh, and look at these beautiful topaz gems – they *have* to go on the veil!"

"That's a lovely idea," said Primrose. She helped Willa pick out the gems, and Blossom soon got to work, embroidering the dress with jewels just like she decorated her cakes.

Meanwhile, Willa made a diamond-daisy necklace and an emerald-nut tiara with the leftover jewels. As she fastened the last emerald nut, she noticed that the sun pouring through the leaf-shaped windows had begun to dim, turning a dusky red colour. Willa realized she'd been so focused she hadn't heard Primrose's cuckoo clock all afternoon. She glanced at the time – it was almost sunset, which meant that the creatures and fairies would need to leave soon.

"Willa, Willa!" called Blossom. "Look. . ."

Willa swung back round to see the magpies very carefully picking the dress up in their beaks. *Oh my fairyness!* It was better than she could have ever hoped for! The dress was made up of shimmering leaves in beautiful green colours, and the jewel-moth silk made each leaf glisten as it moved in the dusky light. A gold-leaf ribbon wrapped about the waist, and the heart-shaped

neckline was edged in silver-star lace. A
pair of hummingbirds held out the train,
which reached halfway across Primrose's
bedroom, and was covered in gorgeous
white and yellow diamonds.

Above the dress, a second pair of hummingbirds dangled the veil, which was spun out of the most delicate caterpillar-silk and sparkled with topaz gems.

"It's incredible!" Willa said, as everyone in the room oohed and aahed. "I just hope that Topaz likes it!"

Chapter 7

Willa woke up early the next morning –
before the birds had even begun their
dawn chorus! Her head buzzed with
excitement about the wedding. She
jumped up out of her palm-leaf hammock
and rushed over to her wardrobe, where
Topaz's dress hung. She grinned – it
looked even more beautiful than it did
last night, sparkling in the light from the
fireflies.

As Willa fluttered along the fairy skyway towards the Tree Palace, birds began waking up and tweeting their dawn songs. Nerves bubbled up in Willa's stomach. Although she thought the dress was wonderful, she still felt nervous about showing it to Topaz. Maybe nothing would compare with the wedding dress that she'd lost. Willa tried to shake the feeling away, and focused instead on carrying the dress as she flew. Willa usually liked to zip about the forest quickly, but today she was being extra careful!

The towering turrets of the jewel-covered palace were soon in sight. Willa slowed down as she crossed one of the oak-leaf drawbridges that connected the palace to the fairy skyway and fluttered into the entrance hall. Topaz was staying in the guest wing of the palace, so Willa flitted over to a knot in the wall and whispered into the wood. She didn't want to disturb the fairy royalty by stomping up all the staircases! She flew up the secret passage, taking care not to bash the dress against the wall. She soon arrived at Topaz's door.

Tap, tap. Willa knocked on the door gently – it was still very early. Topaz might not even be up yet! But the doorway was flung open right away. "Willa, it's you! I'm so glad you're here – I've barely slept a fairy wink. I

can't stop thinking about the wedding.
I even asked one of the fairy-helpers to
make me some daisy-milk tea, but that
didn't help!"

Willa fluttered in through the doorway,
the dress in her arms.

Topaz gasped, her blue eyes widening.
"Is that what I think it is? You really
found me a dress?"

"I did even better than that," said
Willa. "The whole forest *made* you one!"

"Oh, oh, oh!" Topaz cried, staring at
the glittering dress that Willa held up.

"You don't like it?" Willa asked her
speechless friend.

Topaz was now opening and closing
her mouth like a goldfish.

"Topaz, say something, please! If you
really hate it, maybe I can make some
adjustments. . ."

The strawberry-blonde fairy gently picked up the leaf fabric of the dress and stroked it. "There's no need to do that. Willa, I LOVE IT."

"Are you sure?" Willa asked.

Topaz nodded like a woodpecker, and a huge smile lit up her face as she opened the jewellery box Willa handed to her with the necklace and tiara inside. "Willa, you're amazing," Topaz murmured.

"It wasn't just me – everyone helped

make it," Willa explained. "I could never have done it by myself."

Topaz took Willa's hand. "That's so generous of everyone. How will I thank them all?"

"That's easy — by giving them the best wedding party ever!" Willa pulled a sparkly container from the pocket of her velvet green dress. "Now we should start getting ready! I've brought shimmer-wing-dust and some fairy-magic varnish to paint your nails."

For the rest of the morning, Willa and Topaz prepared for the wedding. Topaz took a long soak in a blueberry-fizz bubble bath while Willa tried on the flower girl outfit Topaz had brought for her. She couldn't stop twirling in the pink satin knee-length dress. She shone like a beautiful jewel! The net skirts underneath made it float out even when she wasn't spinning, and she adored the white lace shawl – for when it got chilly after sunset.

One of the fairy-helpers – tiny four-winged fairies who helped at the palace – brought in sparkling heather juice and sandwiches filled with juniper jam. When Topaz emerged from the fairy bathroom wrapped in her fluffy pink dandelion-seed bathrobe, the two fairies tucked in hungrily. "Ooh, yum!" said Topaz as she wiped crumbs from her face.

The two fairies chatted as Willa carefully painted Topaz's toenails and fingernails. Topaz told Willa about the lovely customers who visited her shop, Sparkle Sensations, and how they were all coming for her wedding today. "They'll be arriving about now," she said. "Eek!"

Willa talked about her forest fairy friends, and how she couldn't wait for them to see Topaz in the dress after all their hard work.

"Then let's not wait a moment longer!" said Topaz, quickly blowing her nails to make sure they were dry. She zipped off into the bathroom with the dress, and Willa sat waiting on the peacock-feather bed.

When Topaz opened the door again, Willa's eyes welled up with tears. Her fairy friend looked *so* very beautiful, and the dress fitted her perfectly. "You look wonderful, Topaz." Willa held out the necklace and tiara. "Let me help you with these."

Willa nestled the emerald- nut tiara in Topaz's hair and fastened the veil. She clasped the diamond- daisy necklace around Topaz's dainty neck.

"There! All ready!" Willa said.

"Not quite!" said Topaz. Willa looked around, panicking. *What have we forgotten?*

Topaz fluttered over to the dressing table, taking care not to trip on her long train, and picked up a shiny turquoise gift box. "This is for you, Willa, to say thank you for being the best flower girl ever."

Willa pushed back the lid. "Oh wow," she muttered. Inside was a gorgeous, sparkling turquoise flower. "Thank you!"

"It's made of topaz – to remind you of being my flower girl. Here, let me fasten it in your hair." Topaz clipped it into Willa's beautiful long dark hair. "Now we're ready," she announced. She took Willa's hand and fluttered to the door. "It's time for me to get married!"

Chapter 8

When Willa and Topaz came out of the
Tree Palace entrance, Willa stopped in
shock. On one of the delicate drawbridges
stood a stunning unicorn. Willa pinched
herself to check she wasn't dreaming.
No – it was real! She'd never seen a
unicorn before, although she knew some
lived in Star Valley. Its coat gleamed a
silvery-white, and magic seemed to sparkle
around its horn.

Topaz fluttered towards the beautiful creature. "I always wanted to travel to my wedding on a unicorn, ever since I was a little girl." She grinned and stroked its shining coat. "But, Willa, I have a question to ask. . . Will you fly behind me to hold my train?"

Willa jumped up in excitement. "Oh yes, of course I will!" The thought of flying behind Topaz and the unicorn on the way to the wedding was almost too much to bear – Willa had never done anything quite so special.

Moments later, Topaz was perched on the great white creature, its wings flapping powerfully. Willa flew behind, holding the end of the train tight in both hands. She had to flutter her own wings very quickly to keep up with the unicorn. As they travelled through the forest above the skyways and sparkling trees, they passed fairies and creatures making their way to the wedding, all dressed up in their finest forest-leaf clothes. Everyone waved and called out to them, making Willa feel like royalty.

"Ooh, look, there's the fairy bride on a unicorn!" said a pink tree squirrel.

"Aaah, and her flower girl's behind her. They both look so pretty!" said a chestnut-haired fairy.

Willa smiled so
hard her face ached,
although she couldn't wave back —
she had to keep a firm grip on the
wedding dress!

Soon they were heading down towards
the forest floor and the unicorn flew
through the trees carefully. It landed
just outside the clearing. Topaz reached
forward to the unicorn's neck and gave it
a gentle kiss.

"Thank you," she said. "That was amazing."

As Topaz fluttered down from the unicorn, Willa listened to the chatter of forest fairies and creatures in the clearing, all eager for the wedding to begin. She and Topaz kept out of sight, waiting for the band to begin playing the special Jewel Forest sacred song – which would be Topaz's cue to walk down the aisle.

"Willa, thank you again for everything you've done," said Topaz. "I couldn't have had this wedding without you!"

Willa smiled at her friend and gave her a gentle hug. Then her pointy forest-fairy ears pricked up. The first bars of the sacred song were playing. "Are you ready?" she asked Topaz.

"Yes – I can't wait!" Topaz turned towards the beautiful clearing and Willa carefully picked up the diamond-covered train. As they walked forward slowly, Willa shook with excitement. The clearing looked even more stunning than yesterday. The silver-willow trees sparkled like stars in the bright sunshine, the petal carpet shimmered and rustled, and pretty butterflies and fireflies danced about around them. Multicoloured dandelion seeds floated in the air like the most delicate confetti. Willa knew at that moment that if she ever got married, this was what she wanted it to be like.

Topaz emerged into the clearing and everyone turned to look, all with giant smiles on their faces. Hundreds of tingles shot up Willa's spine as she tiptoed forward, holding out Topaz's beautiful train. When they arrived at the front of the altar, Topaz joined her fairy groom, who was dressed in a holly-leaf top hat and smart suit. He looked very handsome.

Willa gave her friend a kiss on the cheek and took a seat in the front row of toadstools.

Topaz and her groom exchanged woven clover rings and said the words of the Forest Fairy For Ever poem to each other. Willa took out a moss-stitch handkerchief and wiped her eyes – they were filled with tears of joy. She was so happy for her friend! Then everyone began applauding loudly, and Topaz and her groom fluttered back down the aisle, grinning from pointy ear to ear. All the guests gathered handfuls of rose petals to throw over them as they passed, and cheers rang out around the clearing.

The rest of the forest wedding was one giant party. First, the bride and groom cut the beautiful cake, which looked even better than Blossom's drawing. The

peppermint-cream leaves glistened and the edible flowers sparkled. Even the chocolate-cake tree trunk shone with delicious chocolate-butter icing. It was the most beautiful cake Blossom had ever made – and it tasted amazing. Light, soft and sweet. Yum!

As everyone munched on the delicious cake, the sun began to dip in the sky, and Willa worried that it might become too dark. But then the flower-shaped lanterns began to glow, one by one, in beautiful rainbow colours. What's more, sparkling jewel moths darted back and forth, shining flashes of multicoloured light everywhere. Now the clearing looked like a true fairy wonderland.

"Come on, everyone!" Pip called through the bellflower microphone as the band switched to a fast-tempo rhythm. "It's time to get dancing!" Nutmeg tapped the drums while the trumpets tooted and the birds tweeted in time.

Willa felt herself being suddenly whisked away – it was Topaz, pulling her to the dance floor. "I want to make sure I get at least one dance with my extra-special flower girl!" she said as she twirled Willa around. Willa loved to dance, and was soon spinning and fluttering across the grove with Topaz.

"Are you having fun?" Willa asked

during a pause in the music.

Topaz spun Willa around once more. "Oh yes, everything is perfect. And just look – I've never seen the forest so happy!"

Willa took in the hundreds of smiling fairies, the grinning tree squirrels and the fluttering butterflies, moths and birds. The whole forest was buzzing with excitement at such a magical day. Willa had to agree – it really was the most perfect woodland wedding ever.

If you enjoyed this

Fashion Fairy Princess

book then why not visit our
magical new website!

- Explore the enchanted world of
  the fashion fairy princesses
- Find out which fairy princess
  you are
- Download sparkly screensavers
- Make your own tiara
- Colour in your own picture frame
  and much more!

fashionfairyprincess.com

Fashion Fairy Princess

Primrose

in Jewel Forest

Turn the page for a sneak peek of the next
Fashion Fairy Princess adventure...

Chapter 1

"Oh, Primrose! Your room looks beautiful," said Fluff Tail as she hopped into Princess Primrose's bedroom. "Thank you so much for inviting me to stay!"

"Not at all, Fluff Tail," said Primrose, putting her arm around the excited bunny rabbit. "Thank *you* for coming! Nutmeg and I just love sleepovers. We are going to have so much fun."

Fluff Tail hadn't been to a sleepover

at the Tree Palace before and she was very excited. The palace was built into an ancient diamond-nut tree in the heart of the magical Jewel Forest. It was where the king and queen of the forest fairies lived with their two beautiful daughters, Princess Primrose and Nutmeg. Fluff Tail had been to parties in the trunk of the Tree Palace but had never been up into the branches, where the royal bedrooms could be found.

Primrose's bedroom was in a branch close to the top of the tree. It had beautiful polished wooden walls and lots of large leaf-shaped windows that looked out on to Jewel Forest. Fluff Tail hopped over to one of the windows and peered out on to the glittering trees below.

"My goodness!" said Fluff Tail. "I've never seen the forest from this high up.

I think I might even be able to see my lovely little house if the clouds weren't quite so low."

"Not quite," said Primrose, laughing and tucking her glossy nut-brown plait neatly between her glittering yellow wings, "but you can certainly see a long way."

"What was that?" said Fluff Tail, looking hard into the darkening forest. "And another one. . . I think I just saw a raindrop. They look very different from up here, don't they? It must be starting to rain."

"Oh, I do hope so!" said Primrose, fluttering to her bunny friend's side. "I love to look out of the window when it rains, especially at night when the moonlight glints through the raindrops and makes them glow like milky-white gemstones."

"That sounds beautiful," said Fluff Tail, smiling.

"It is," said Primrose excitedly, "and it's even better when the wind blows, too! It rushes through the branches and around the trunk, making a beautiful whistling sound, like lots of forest fairy flutes playing all at once. It's magical and—"

Primrose stopped as her bedroom door swung open and an enormous tray, piled high with delicious sleepover treats, entered the room. Fluttering behind, and almost hidden by the huge tray she was carrying, was a small fairy with choppy nut-brown hair and glittering orange wings, who was wearing leaf-patterned pyjamas with fluffy slippers.

It was Primrose's little sister, Nutmeg.

"Hello, Fluff Tail! I'm so glad you came," said Nutmeg, placing the rose-coloured wooden tray on Primrose's bed. "I asked the palace kitchen to make your favourite carrot cupcakes."

"I hope you didn't go to any trouble, Nutmeg," said Fluff Tail, hopping over to the bed and eyeing the tray of yummy-looking cakes hungrily.

"No trouble at all!" said Nutmeg, smiling and popping one of the orange-frosted cakes into her mouth. "Primrose and I love them, too."

"Ooh, is that a bottle of forest fizz?" asked Primrose, pointing at a glittery glass bottle. "I do hope it's ruby-currant flavour."

"It is!" said Nutmeg, handing her a cup.

"My favourite!" said Primrose. "Fluff Tail, have you tried it before?"

"It's delicious!" said Fluff Tail, giggling and twitching her little pink nose. "And I love the way the bubbles make my nose tickle."

When they had finished the delicious

tray of goodies, the full-up fairies flopped back on to Primrose's bed, and Fluff Tail let out a groan, looking at the empty plates.

"I'm so full," she said, rubbing her round tummy with her soft silvery paws.

"Me, too!" said Primrose, laughing. "I suppose we won't be needing a midnight feast after all."

"Mmm, no. . ." said Nutmeg, smiling sleepily.

"Good thing, too," said Fluff Tail. "My cousins Eloise and Silver are coming to stay with me at my burrow tomorrow, and I want to be home early to get everything ready for them."

Fluff Tail lived in a burrow called Sapphire Lodge. It was dug into the roots of a beautiful sapphire tree a short walk from the Tree Palace.

"Listen to the rain now," said Primrose.

"It sounds like there might be a storm. We'd better close the shutters on the windows before we go to sleep."

"I hope it's a storm," said Nutmeg. "There's nothing nicer than being all tucked up and cosy, listening to the wind howling outside. It's so exciting."

"Don't you get a bit scared, being this high up when the wind is blowing so hard?" asked Fluff Tail.

"Not at all," said Nutmeg. "This tree has been here for ever! It'll take more than a little storm to blow it— Eeeeek! What was that?"

Nutmeg wrapped her slim freckled arms around the bunny's soft body, startled by a sudden crashing sound outside.

"Nutmeg!" said Primrose, laughing gently at her funny little sister. "That was just a bit of thunder."

"I know *that*," said Nutmeg, blushing, a little embarrassed for having made such a fuss.

Primrose walked over and held her sister's hand. "Perhaps you'd better sleep in here with us tonight," she said gently.

"Oh yes! Please can I?" said Nutmeg, cheering up instantly. "Not because I'm scared, of course, but I do hate missing out on all the fun. I'll go and get the hammocks!"

Get creative with the fashion fairy princesses in these magical sticker-activity books!

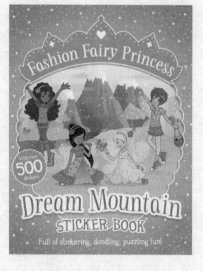